W9-BDI-965

Jenny Reen
AND THE
Jack Muh Lantern

written by IRENE SMALLS

illustrated by KEINYO WHITE

ATHENEUM BOOKS FOR YOUNG READERS

For all the beautiful Black women in my family:
Louise, Jenny, Aunt Myrle, Toye, Mary, Myrtle, Cheryl, Yvonne, Dawn, Dana,
Momo, Nyeilla, Marina, Shirelle, Patricia, Kajani, Carolyn, Susan, Valerie,
Grandma Mary, Evonna, Star of Asia, Chante, Ruby, Chrisondria, Lisa, Janeka,
Germanique, Laura, Hazel, and "I Love You, Black Child." —I. S.

For my parents and family, my godchildren Michael and Alexandra,
and finally for Mahler B. Ryder, who pushed me to become a professional
and conscientious illustrator. —K. W.

Atheneum Books for Young Readers
An imprint of Simon & Schuster Children's Publishing Division
1230 Avenue of the Americas
New York, New York 10020

Text copyright © 1996 by Irene Smalls
Illustrations copyright © 1996 by Keinyo White

All rights reserved including the right of reproduction
in whole or in part in any form.

Book design by Ann Bobco
The text of this book is set in Journal Bold.
The illustrations are rendered in oil.

Manufactured in the United States of America

First Edition

10 9 8 7 6 5 4 3 2 1

Library of Congress Cataloging in Publication Data

Smalls, Irene.
Jenny Reen and the Jack Muh Lantern / by Irene Smalls ;
illustrated by Keinyo White. — 1st ed.
p. cm.
"This story is based on African-American folktales and oral histories" —P.
Summary: Sister Louisa, who cares for Jenny Reen while her parents work in
the field, warns the young slave girl about a monster, known from long-told tales,
who comes out on Halloween.
Includes bibliographical references.
ISBN 0-689-31875-8
[1. Slavery—Fiction. 2. Afro-Americans—Fiction. 3. Halloween—Fiction.]
I. White, Keinyo, ill. II. Title.
PZ7.S63915Je   1996   94-14454
[Fic]dc—20

AUTHOR'S NOTE

This story is about a time when black people's knowledge was created by imagination and passed on by tongue. It was against the law to teach a black person to read and write, so the whys of the world were reasoned by their hearts and minds. This story is based on authentic African-American folktales, songs, and oral histories found in the following sources:

Botkin, Benjamin A., ed. *Lay My Burden Down: A Folk History of Slavery*. Chicago: University of Chicago Press, 1965.

Campbell, Edward D.C. and Kym Rice, eds. *Before Freedom Came: African-American Life in the Antebellum South*. Charlottesville: University of Virginia Press, 1991.

Dorson, Richard M., ed. *American Negro Folktales*. Greenwich, Conn.: Fawcett World Library, 1956.

Hurmence, Belinda. *Before Freedom*. New York: Penguin Group, 1990.

Jackson, Bruce, ed. *The Negro and His Folktale*. Austin, Texas: American Folklore Society, 1967.

Once upon a time, when the great mountains were high, before they were pebbled apart into the sandy beach that we are standing on today, before today's present time of laughter, there was a time of great tears. Tears that ran so full and so deep that rivers were made that still flow. In this time of tears, our fathers' fathers' father and mothers' mothers' mother worked rain-wet and sun-dry, sunup to sundown. Each rising sun meant another hard day.

In this hardest of hard times there was still joy because there were children, children with round cheeks and round curls. Such a child was Jenny Reen.

Jenny Reen's daddy, Charles Hubert, and her mommy, Mary Ellen, worked in the cotton fields, leaving Jenny Reen under the watchful eye of Sister Louisa, the slave quarter roots woman. Some said that Sister Louisa was a witch, for she worked with roots and plants to make healing potions. But Sister Louisa was kind, and children were her special joy.

On the day before Halloween Jenny Reen was strutting
around the slave quarter feeling fit as a fiddle. The
quarter's rude wooden cabins, fenced in by the overseer's
house, the henhouse, the barn, and the cotton house was
Jenny Reen's world.

Sister Louisa was busily stitching a dress for Jenny Reen's new doll baby. She carefully reached into her breast pocket and took out her yearly ration of three buttons.

She sewed two of the buttons on the doll's face. Then she returned the last button to her pocket. Sister Louisa slipped a small *asofedica* bag around the doll's neck to ward off sickness, and she handed it to Jenny Reen.

As the small girl cradled the doll, a dark cloud rolled across the sky. Jenny Reen looked up and asked, "Sister Louisa, what is thunder?"

"Chile, thunder is the movin' of God's feets across the sky. And the lightnin' is the wrinklin' of his eye," Sister Louisa answered.

"Sister Louisa,
when will I'se be free?"
Jenny Reen asked.

"When you can read your title clear to the mansion in the sky," Sister Louisa whispered. "Now hush, chile, those words can bring you trouble past tellin'."

Later, as the sun slipped slowly down the sky, Sister Louisa said,"When day clean come, it's All Hallows' Eve. On Halloween witches, ghosties, and all manner of beasties is about. But the worsest creature of them all is the Jack Muh Lantern."

"Jack Muh Lantern? Whatsa Jack Muh Lantern, Sister Louisa?" Jenny Reen asked fearfully as she held her doll close to her.

Well, chile, the Jack Muh Lantern is this terrible creature who wanders dusk to dawn with its lantern, through woods and marshes seeking to lead people to they's destruction. The Jack Muh Lantern is a hideous little bein' somewhat like people in form, but covered with hair like a dog. It has great googly google eyes and no lips, just a big wide gash, open from ear to ear. In height it ain't more than four or five feet and it is skinnier 'n a board. But oh, the Jack Muh Lantern has magic powers. It has the power of locomotion. You can't overtake it or escape from it, once it got you in its power, for it can leap higher'n a grasshopper to most any distance. And its strength is beyond all human resistance. Ten men couldn't rassle a Jack Muh Lantern to the dirt. It don't bite or tear its victims. No, it's worser than that. The Jack Muh Lantern leads you into the bogs and marshes and leaves you there to slowly sink and slowly die."

"Oh, ohh," Jenny Reen said, her eyes as big as hoecakes.

"There ain't no power here on earth to save you once the Jack Muh Lantern's got you in its clutches. The onliest thing that a body can do to protect hisself is take off his outer garment and put it on again inside out. Then the foul fiend is instantly deprived of all power to harm," Sister Louisa finished.

"Wells, I'm staying away from that creature," Jenny Reen said, shuddering. She went back to playing with her new baby doll.

In the distance Jenny Reen could hear singing:
"I know moonrise, I know star rise
Lay dis body down
I walk in de moonlight, I walk in de starlight
To lay dis body down."

The slaves were returning from the cotton fields. Jenny Reen saw her mother and father marching in the line.

"Sister, I'll sees you in the morning. I'se gonna remember 'bout that Jack Muh Lantern," Jenny Reen said.

The next afternoon, Sister Louisa said to Jenny Reen, "Chile, I gots to send you on an errand. I wants you to go to Miss Cathereen's and ask if she could see her way clear to give me a pinch of sassafras roots. And chile, trouble is looking for you! Stay on the path an' out of them woods!" Sister Louisa warned.

"Yes'm. I ain't lookin' for no trouble doin's with no Jack Muh Lantern," said a very meek Jenny Reen.

Jenny Reen started down the road with one thing on her mind; "Miss Cathereen's, Miss Cathereen's." But it wasn't long before she started to wander.

"Huh, that ole Jack Muh Lantern best stay away from me," she boasted. Feeling brave, she started singing:

"Old Black Bull come
    down de hollow
He shake his tail, you
    hear him bellow
When he bellow he jar
    de river
he paw de earth, he
    make it quiver
Who zen John, Who za
Who zen John, Who za."

She wandered boldly into the woods. In the cool of the woods there was a beautiful red flower. And then a butterfly started to tease, playing butterfly tag.

After a while Jenny
Reen noticed the sun
sliding down the sky.
"Oh no," she said.
"Sister Louisa is goin'
to be so cross with me."
Then she gasped, "It's
Halloween." Her heart
started pounding.

Jenny Reen hurried up, but
which way had she come? Was it
toward that tree or through
that small clearing? She wasn't sure.
She stopped and crouched near a
large rock. She hadn't heard any
footsteps but her skin began to
crawl. She felt someone was near.

Jenny Reen looked behind her: nobody there. She looked to the right side: nobody there. She looked to the left side: nobody there.

She turned to face front again, and there it was! A wild-looking, mannish creature with bulging eyes: the Jack Muh Lantern!

Jenny Reen turned, picked up her heels and took off. But there it was still in front of her!

Jenny Reen was scared. She tried to remember what it was that Sister Louisa had told her about the onliest way to get away from the Jack Muh Lantern. But, she couldn't catch her breath, she couldn't think! She kept running, dipping and dodging this way then that. But it was no use. That Jack Muh Lantern was always there.

Finally, she couldn't run anymore. The bushes and brambles
had torn her shirt. Her arms, legs, and face were all scratched
up. Her bare feet were bleeding. The Jack Muh Lantern came
closer and closer, eager to get its prey.

The Jack Muh Lantern was so close that Jenny Reen could see
clearly into its googly google eyes, eyes filled with delight that
its prey was ripe for the kill. It rolled its eyes around in their
bloody red sockets.

Jenny Reen was terrified. But Sister Louisa had said: "There's always a way out of no way." Thinking of Sister Louisa calmed her. Then Jenny Reen remembered what to do.

Jenny Reen swiftly took off her jacket and put in on inside out. At that same moment the Jack Muh Lantern reached out to touch her. But it touched her too late.

"Eheeeeeheheh!" it screeched. "Eheeeeeheheh!" And it ran off toward the marshes still screaming, "Eheeeeeheheh! Eheeeeeheheh!

Jenny Reen ran the opposite way. She ran and ran until she could run no more. Then she collapsed at the bottom of a large moss-covered tree. She wanted to lie there on the cool moss forever, but slowly she stood up. She had to find her way out of the woods.

Crying as she walked, with her jacket on inside out, Jenny Reen found the search party that had been sent to look for her.

Jenny Reen's mother grabbed her. "My baby girl is all right!" she cried. Her daddy kissed her tear-stained cheeks.

Sister Louisa handed Jenny Reen her baby doll. She held Jenny Reen last and the longest.

Jenny Reen sobbed, "Sister Louisa, I'se sorry. Do you still loves me?"

Sister Louisa answered, "Chile, I couldn't loves you any more if you was the worsest or the bestest one or about the levelest one. If I loved you any more my heart would break."

Jenny Reen's daddy picked her up. Sister Louisa and Mary Ellen were on either side. The rest of the search party followed, singing:

"Dere's no rain to wet you
Oh yes, I want to go home
Dere's no sun to burn you
Oh yes, I want to go home
Oh yes, I want to go home."

D.C. PUBLIC LIBRARY

3 1172 03614 0937

LAR.
JUV.

RECEIVED DEC - 8 2014

J
SMA

Holiday

4/98